www.FlowerpotPress.com
CHC-0909-0481
ISBN: 978-1-4867-1658-6
Made in China/Fabriqué en Chine

Rumble, Rumble, Grumble, Grumble

Sounds from the Sky

Written by Jennifer Shand
Illustrated by Barbara Vagnozzi

Did you hear that?

I hear rumble, rumble, rumble and grumble, grumble, grumble!

Then I hear a sudden **crash** and a **boom**, **boom**, **boom**!

What is that?

I hear **pitter**, **pitter**, **pitter** **and** pat, pat, pat with a **drip**, **drip**, **drip** and a **splat**, **splat**, **splat!**

What is that?

It's the rain pitter-pattering
as it splats on the ground!

I hear whirl, whirl, whirl, whish, whish, whish and flurry, flurry, flurry!

I hear **crackle, crackle, crackle** and **rustle, rustle, rustle!**

What is that?

It's the wind whirl, whirl, whirling as it rustles through the forest!

I hear a buzz, buzz, buzz going zigzag, zigzag this way and that way!

There is a bustle of **bzzz, bzzz, bzzz** and whirr, whirr, whirr!

What is that?

I hear chirp, chirp, chirp and tweet, tweet, tweet

with lots of

chitter, chitter, chatter and **whistle, whistle, whistle!**

What is that?

It's the songbirds chirping and whistling a sweet song!

I hear a hoot, hoot, hoot with a whooo, whooo, whooo!

There's a **flip**, **flip**, **flap** and a **flap**, **flip**, **flip**!

What is that?

It's the owls in the treetops hooting and whoooing as they flip and flap their wings!

I hear **pitter**, **pitter**, **rumble**, **rumble** and **whirl**, **whirl**, **whirl**

with a
**buzz, buzz,
chirp, chirp**
and a hoot,
hoot, hoot!

What is that?

It's all the sounds from the sky on the first day of spring!

Wait...
Did you hear that?